For Mark

Published by Delacorte Press
Bantam Doubleday Dell Publishing Group, Inc.
666 Fifth Avenue, New York, New York 10103

First published in Great Britain by Julia MacRae Books,
a division of Walker Books Ltd., London

20 19 18 17 16 15 14 13 12 11 10 9 8 7 6 5 4 3 2 1

Coming
ready
or
not

Library of Congress Cataloging in Publication Data
Thompson, Carol.
In my bedroom / Carol Thompson.   p.   cm.
"First published in Great Britain by Julia MacRae Books in 1990"–T.p. verso.
Summary: A young pig's bedroom is a place in which to play, dress, and sleep.
ISBN 0-385-29857-9
[1. Bedrooms–Fiction. 2. Pigs–Fiction.]
I. Title.
PZZ.T37142310   1990   89-31721
[E]–dc19   CIP
                                         AC

Manufactured in Italy
First U.S.A. printing
March 1990
10 9 8 7 6 5 4 3 2 1

IN MY BEDROOM

ready!

Carol Thompson

Delacorte
Press

In my bedroom I can
find all sorts of things —

a bed,

a chair,

a toy chest.

The toy chest is full of things
to play with —

a duck,

a train,

some bricks,

and a hat.

My chair can be
anything —

a lookout post,

something to drive,

a secret place.

I can even sit on it.

I keep my clothes in a special place

with a rail to hang things from
and shoes on the floor.

It makes a good hiding place.

The shelves are for my favorite things —

a coin bank,   books,

and all my crayons
for drawing.

My bed is just right
for me.

It has a pillow,   a light beside it,

a potty underneath,   and a soft cover.

I dress in my bedtime
clothes —

pajamas,

slippers,

and a bathrobe
with a cord.

When I go to bed

I take my best friend with me.